PENELOPE
AND HER
ROCKS

A STORY ABOUT ACCEPTING YOURSELF

Written And Illustrated By
Pascale Beauboeuf Roane

Balboa Press books may be ordered through booksellers or by contacting:

Scripture quotations marked NIV are taken from the Holy Bible, New International Version®. NIV®. Copyright © 1973, 1978, 1984 by International Bible Society. Used by permission of Zondervan. All rights reserved. [Biblica]

Balboa Press
A Division of Hay House
1663 Liberty Drive
Bloomington, IN 47403
www.balboapress.com
1 (877) 407-4847

ISBN: 978-1-5043-6283-2 (sc)
ISBN: 978-1-5043-6282-5 (e)

Library of Congress: 2016911829

Print information available on the last page.

Balboa Press rev. date: 12/14/2018

BALBOA.
PRESS
A DIVISION OF HAY HOUSE

Dedicated
With Love To
Kathy Vega
Simran Singh
AND
Abishai
Ben Reuben

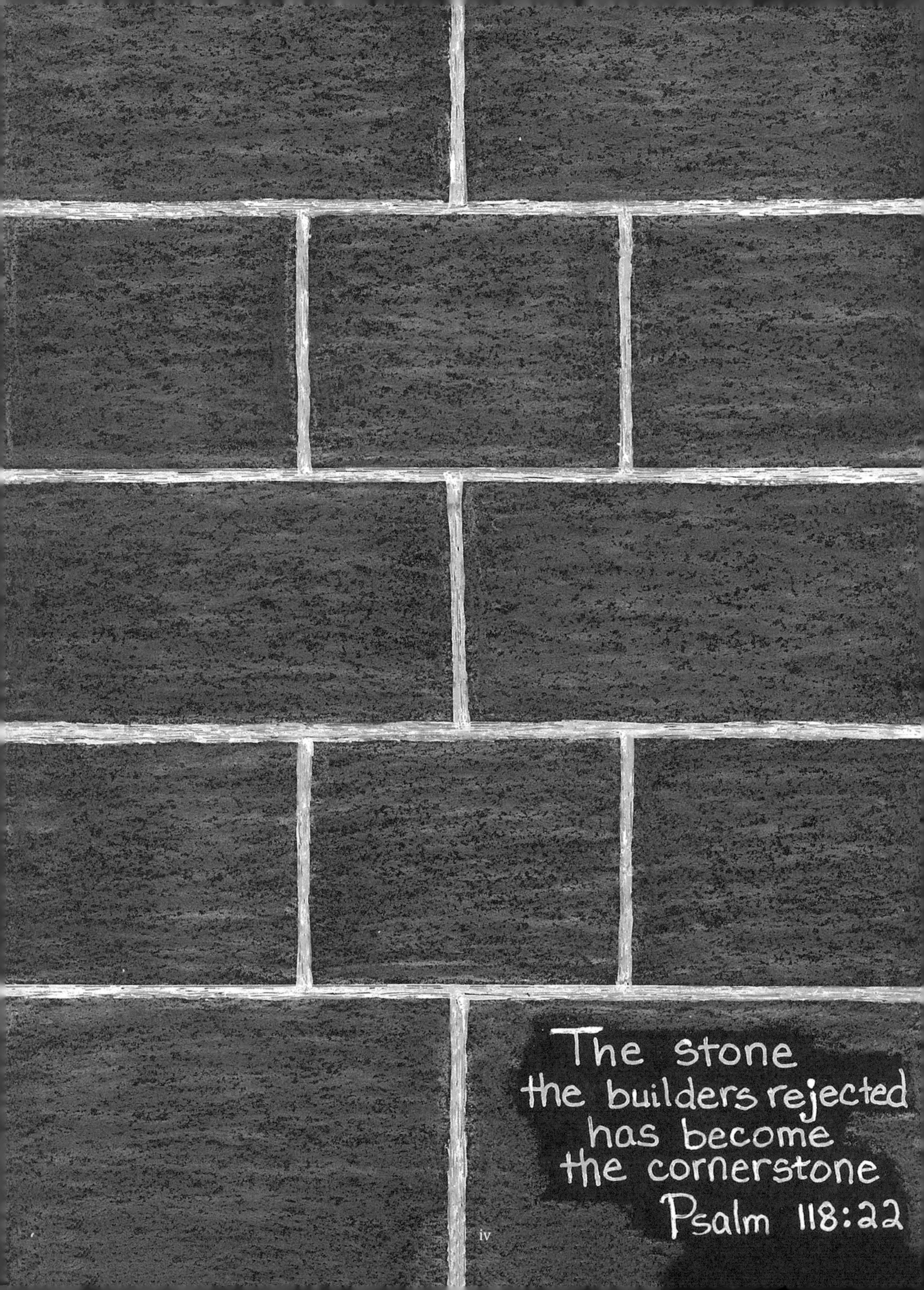

The stone
the builders rejected
has become
the cornerstone
Psalm 118:22

Once upon a time there was a girl named Penelope who loved to play with rocks. She was fascinated by their different shapes, sizes, and the way they felt in her hands.

All the children living in Cookie Cutterville liked to play with dolls and cars but Penelope enjoyed digging for stones which were added to what had become a huge rock collection. This was her favorite thing to do. She could actually feel love inside of the Earth.

Finding rocks made Penelope happy and while she inspired some people with her unique ways, the rulers of the town did not understand her. They would frown at her dirty face and clothes while saying, "Here in Cookie Cutterville, we don't play in the dirt."

After putting on her nicest outfit one day, she was told "Penelope, you look so nice. Please stay away from the rocks. Otherwise, we will have to banish you to The Place Outside The Lines."

She tried. She really did try to resist putting her hands deep within the rich soil to touch her precious rocks but it was like the Earth was calling her name and she could smell its nature. Before long, she was knee deep in a wonderful experience of dirt and rocks.

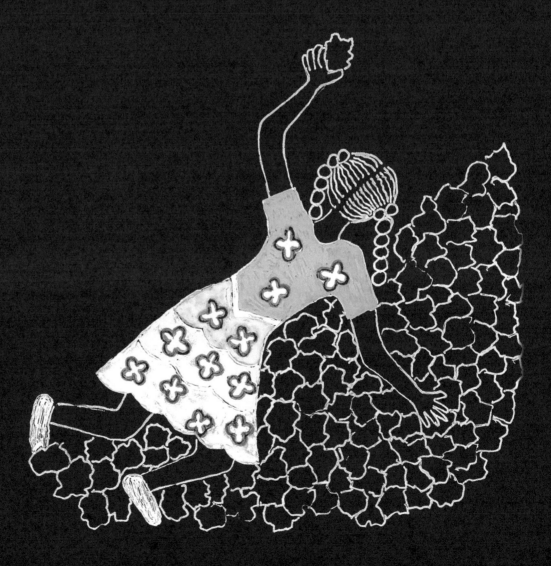

Penelope heard "We warned you Penelope but you didn't listen! You leave us no choice but to send you to The Place Outside The Lines. What do you have to say for yourself?"

Penelope thought for a while and then asked "Can I take my rocks with me?"

"Oh Penelope, when will you learn?"

BUS DEPOT

Later that day she was banished to The Place Outside The Lines. Upon arriving, one of the town's people approached Penelope and said "You don't look like you belong Outside The Lines. Why are you here?"

She replied "I like to play with rocks."

The Place Outside The Lines was inhabited with people, animals and plants that did not look happy and she wondered why. Blessed with keen intuition, Penelope dipped her hand into the soil and felt an untapped richness. She understood in that moment that she was there to show the inhabitants their worth and to love.

Compassion flowed from Penelope's heart for the droopy, withering plants all around her. The strong relationship she had with nature told her exactly what to do.

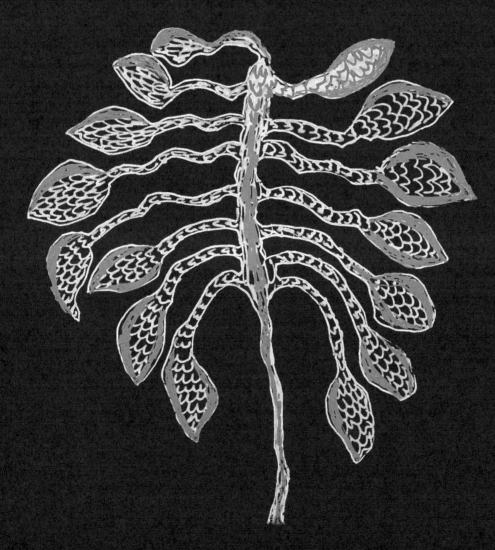

Penelope dug holes and replanted the greenery.
She watered them and positioned rocks all
around so the support they needed was in place.
They then started to grow and flourish.

The animals across the land were panting
because they were parched for water.

Penelope found rocks to throw into a watering hole.
As the rocks piled up, the water rose to the top
and the animals drank to their hearts content.

The men were survivors who only knew how to
do battle. They felt enraged because they did not
know how to use their strength productively.
They wanted their lives to have meaning.

Penelope looked for the biggest rocks she could find to make armor and weapons with. She gave them to the men and showed them how to channel their feelings. She spoke with them about fighting with dignity and inspired them to become the protectors of the village.

The women were bitter. Their hearts had become
cold and they cut each other with their words.
They had forgotten how beautiful they were.

Penelope looked for the prettiest and most colorful rocks she could find. She made earring and pendants with them, and then gave the jewelry to the women as gifts. The nurturing Earth energy contained in the rocks melted their hardness away. Their hearts could feel, their words became healing, and the women knew they were beautiful again.

The village elders were scared and full of doubt.
They didn't know what to believe in.

Penelope looked for the smoothest pebbles she could find. With them, she made strings of prayer beads and gave them to the elders. She spoke with them about intentions from the heart and ways to create peaceful vibrations. The elders prayed for guidance. Their beliefs were strengthened and they found faith again.

The boys were bored. Their need for adventure and intellectual stimulation had been misjudged as "bad behavior".

Penelope looked for a handful of the roundest rocks she could find. She shaped each one into a perfect circle so that the boys could play marbles with each other. They formed teams and started a tournament. This taught them about the art of strategy, building confidence and how to win.

The girls had been misunderstood by people who thought they knew who they were supposed to be.

Each of these girls had been blessed with a remarkable purpose. They simply desired to follow their hearts and be true to themselves. Penelope gave them the greatest gift she had. She taught them to dig and find richness within the Earth. From this, they learned how to look inside of themselves and discover their own personal treasures.

Whenever the people of the village tried to meet as a group, they would talk over each other.

Penelope looked for a specific kind of rock that glowed when it was held. She told the community that the person holding the rock would be the one to speak and when finished, he or she would pass the rock to the next speaker. This is how they learned to take turns and listen to one another.

The people in the village didn't know how to
be friends. All of their doors were closed.

Penelope gave everyone a thin triangular friendship rock to put under their door. This rock would hold the door open and let others know when it was okay to come in. This is how people in the village started building caring relationships.

The village originally called The Place Outside The Lines became known as The Place Where Love Lives. It transformed into an environment where everybody wanted to be because people were accepted and encouraged there. They just needed someone with vision to show them how to use what they had in a productive way.

The inhabitants knew that they belonged and that they mattered. They became the heroes, protectors, communicators, advocates, healers, priests, reverends, strategists, winners, leaders and role models of the world.

Penelope became both an alchemist and an archeologist. She continues to travel all over the planet looking inside of the Earth for precious artifacts while teaching people how to search their souls to find their own treasures.

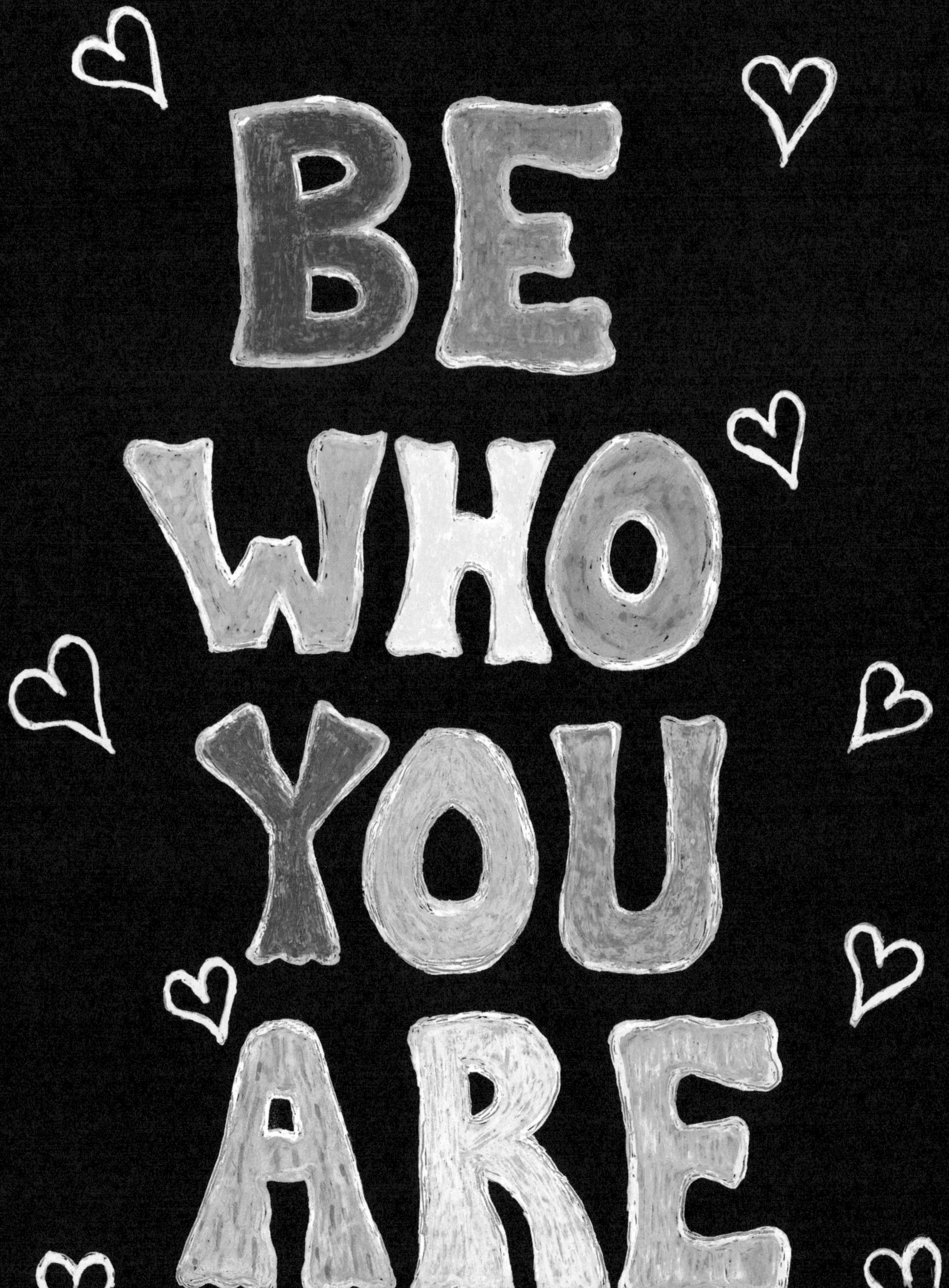
BE
WHO
YOU
ARE

Printed in the United States
By Bookmasters